KAY THOMPSON'S ELOISE

Eloise's Pirate Adventure

STORY BY I

ILLUSTRATED BY Tammie Lyon

Ready-to-Read

Aladdin

NEW YORK · LONDON · TORONTO · SYDNEY

ALADDIN PAPERBACKS
An imprint of Simon & Schuster Children's Publishing Division
1230 Avenue of the Americas, New York, NY 10020
Copyright © 2007 by the Estate of Kay Thompson
All rights reserved, including the right of reproduction in whole or in part in any form.
"Eloise" and related marks are trademarks of the Estate of Kay Thompson.
READY-TO-READ, ALADDIN PAPERBACKS, and related logo are
registered trademarks of Simon & Schuster, Inc.
The text of this book was set in Century Old Style.
Manufactured in the United States of America
First Aladdin Paperbacks edition September 2007
6 8 10 9 7
Library of Congress Control Number 2007921380
ISBN-13: 978-1-4169-4979-4
ISBN-10: 1-4169-4979-8
0912 LAK

My name is Eloise.
I am a city child.
I live at The Plaza Hotel.

I love to play dress-up.
Sometimes I am a princess.

Sometimes I am a dinosaur.

Sometimes
I am Nanny.

Sometimes
I am Weenie.

Today I am a pirate.
Oh I love, love, love pirates!

I wiggle out of
my socks.
I put on the
pirate hat.

And the eye patch.

And the sword.

And the boots.

Weenie is my
first mate.
"Weenie," I say,
"it is time
to set sail!"

"There is treasure to be found," I say.
Does Nanny have the treasure?

"No, no, no, Eloise," says Nanny. "There is no treasure under my chair!"

Does Room Service have the treasure?

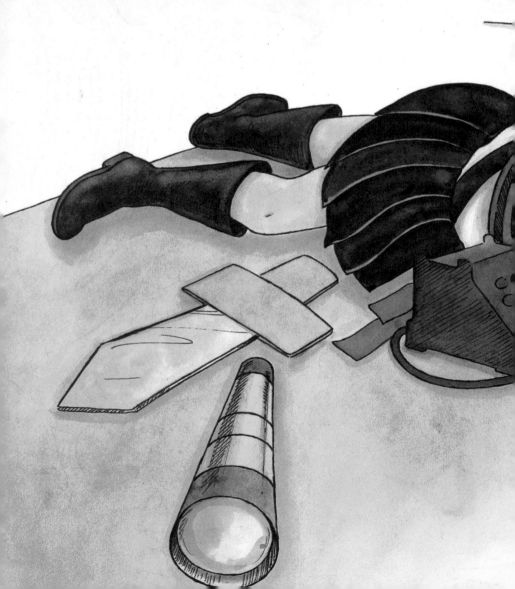

"Room Service," I say,
"please send up the
treasure at once!"

"No, no, no, Eloise,"
says Room Service.

Does Chef have the treasure?
Weenie and I sail down
to the kitchen.

"No, no, no, Eloise," says Chef. "There is no treasure in my pots and pans!"

"I know," I say. "The manager has the treasure!"

Weenie and I make a map.

It is a very dangerous climb down to the lobby.

"Do you have the treasure?"
I say to the manager.

"Why, Eloise," says
the manager, "I may. . . ."

"Will these chocolate coins do?"
"Why, yes!" I say.

Oh I love, love, love pirates!